Before reading

Look at the book cover
Ask, "What do you thin

Turn to the **Key Words**
the child. Draw their a
the tall letters and those that have a tail.

During reading

Offer plenty of support and praise as the child reads the story.
Listen carefully and respond to events in the text.

When a **Key Word** is used for the first time, it is also shown at
the bottom of the page. If the child hesitates over a word, point
to the **New Key Words** box and practise reading it together.
If the word is phonically decodable, you can sound out the
letters and blend the sounds to read the word ("d-o-g, dog").
Praise the child for their effort, then return to the story.

Pause every few pages and ask questions to check the child's
understanding of what they have read. If they begin to lose
concentration, stop reading and save the page for later.

Celebrate the child's achievement and come back to the
story the next day.

After reading

After reading this book, ask, "Did you enjoy the story? What did
you like about it?" Encourage the child to share their opinions.

Use the comprehension questions on page 54 to check the
child's understanding and recall of the text.

Ladybird

Series Consultant: Professor David Waugh
With thanks to Kulwinder Maude

LADYBIRD BOOKS

UK | USA | Canada | Ireland | Australia
India | New Zealand | South Africa

Ladybird Books is part of the Penguin Random House group of companies
whose addresses can be found at global.penguinrandomhouse.com.
www.penguin.co.uk   www.puffin.co.uk   www.ladybird.co.uk

Penguin
Random House
UK

Original edition of Key Words with Peter and Jane first published by Ladybird Books Ltd 1964
Series updated 2023
This book first published 2023
002

Text copyright © Ladybird Books Ltd, 1964, 2023
Illustrations by Gustavo Mazali
Illustrations copyright © Ladybird Books Ltd, 2023

Printed in China

The authorized representative in the EEA is Penguin Random House Ireland,
Morrison Chambers, 32 Nassau Street, Dublin D02 YH68

A CIP catalogue record for this book is available from the British Library

ISBN: 978-0-241-51091-9

All correspondence to:
Ladybird Books
Penguin Random House Children's
One Embassy Gardens, 8 Viaduct Gardens, London SW11 7BW

MIX
Paper from
responsible sources
FSC® C018179
FSC
www.fsc.org

Key Words

with Peter and Jane

7a

The best picture

Based on the original
Key Words with Peter and Jane
reading scheme and research by William Murray

Original edition written by William Murray
This edition written by James Clements
Illustrated by Gustavo Mazali

Key Words

about again as ask

brother cafe city drink

eat how know more

museum now other park

picture really river saw

sister so something soon

street take their top

who window

brother

cafe

city

drink

eat

museum

park

picture

river

sister

street

window

Jane had something she wanted to show her brother.

"The museum wants to see who can take the best picture of an animal," she said.

"We can take good pictures of animals," said Peter. "We can take one for the museum!"

New Key Words

something   brother   museum

who   take   picture

"Mum, can we ask you something?" asked Peter.
"Can we take a picture of an animal for the museum?"

"Yes, you can," said Mum.
"You take really good pictures. Who knows, you might win!"

Mum had something for Peter and Jane.

"Do you know how to take a picture with this?" asked Mum.

"Yes," Jane said. "We know how."

"Take a picture out of the window to check you really do know how," Mum said.

Peter and Jane walked up the stairs. They looked out of Peter's window.

"I saw a bird near the top of that tree," said Peter.

"There it is again!" said Jane. "Quick, take a picture. Press that bit on the top."

"That bird was really quick!" Peter said to his sister as they looked out of the window.

"Let's take pictures of some other animals," said Jane.

"I know – the park might be a good spot to take pictures," said Peter.

"Yes! Let's ask Mum to take us to the park now," Jane said.

New Key Words

sister   as   other   park   now

Jane asked Mum, who said, "The park is good, but I know one other spot we can get to on the train. How about the top of the hill? There will be more animals there."

"Is there a cafe at the top of the hill?" asked Peter.

"No, there's not a cafe," said Mum, as she packed something for them to eat and drink.

New Key Words

about   more   cafe   eat   drink

Peter and Jane walked down their high street with their mum and their dog, Tess.

"Peter, there is a bird hopping about," said Jane. "Take a picture again, now!"

The bird hopped down the street. "I can't get a good picture," said Peter.

"You will see other animals at the top of the hill," said Mum. "We will get there soon."

21

They walked to the train station at the top of the high street.

As Mum paid for the train, Peter and Jane had a drink.

"Some trains go to the city, and other trains go near Pippa's farm," Jane said.

"So we must take one to the farm," said Peter.

New Key Words

city   so

On the train, Peter and his sister sat near the window. They looked out at the streets.

"Who wants something to eat?" asked Mum.

They had fruit to eat and water to drink.

"How soon will we get there?" asked Peter.

"Soon," said Mum. "This train is really quick."

New Key Words

They saw more and more trees
out of the train window.

"It is really green here. It is not
like the streets in the city,"
said Jane.

"Yes, it's as green as the park!"
said Peter.

"I saw some horses out of the window!" said Peter.

"Who wants to take a picture now?" asked Mum.

It was Jane's turn, but the train was so quick that she had to wait. "I can't get a good picture," she said.

"There will be other animals at the top of the hill," said Peter.

New Key Words

29

Soon, their train was near Pippa's farm, and they jumped off.

"Can we look for animals in the river?" asked Peter.

"We must start our walk now," said Mum. "We'll pass the river again on our walk down."

They walked past Pippa's farm.

Peter saw some cows as they walked. "Let's take a picture of them for the museum," he said.

"Who wants to take the picture?" asked Mum. But the cows stayed near the trees, so Jane and Peter started walking again.

"I saw something good,"
Jane said.

She wanted to take a picture
of the sheep. "They look really
little in the picture," she said.

"Soon, we will be at the top of
the hill," said Mum. "We can have
something to eat and drink there.
We will see some other animals
on the walk down."

At the top of the hill, Jane, Peter and Mum had things to eat and drink from their lunchboxes as Tess played about.

From the top of the hill, they saw the river, Pippa's farm and the city. All the things looked really little from up high.

"Look!" said Peter. "I saw some rabbits. I will take a picture!"

Tess saw the rabbits. She jumped about and barked at them, so the rabbits hopped off.

"Tess!" said Jane, as Tess jumped about again.

Peter and Jane saw the river again.

"I saw a fish swimming in the river!" Peter said to his sister.

"I saw more than one," Jane said to her brother.

"Who will take the picture now?" asked Mum. It was Jane's turn again.

New Key Words

41

Soon, they saw more fish in
the river.

But now Tess had seen the fish!
She started to bark.

"Tess!" yelled Jane. "I can't take
the picture now."

"Not again, Tess!" said Mum.
"Rabbits on the hill and now fish
in the river!"

"It will be the end of our trip really soon," said Mum. "I don't know where to spot other animals for the picture now."

They all had to go home on the other train. Now, their train was going to the city.

They sat near the window again.

45

Peter and Jane walked along their high street with Mum.

"How will we take a picture for the museum now?" Jane asked her brother.

"Don't be sad, Jane," said Mum. "Who wants to get something to eat and drink from that cafe?"

Peter, Jane and Mum sat down at the cafe. They asked for some really big buns.

Tess saw their buns and really wanted one.

"Don't look at my bun, Tess!" said Peter. "You can't take it."

"I will take a picture of Tess, as she looks really sweet," said Jane.

New Key Words

49

At home, Peter and Jane looked at their pictures for the museum.

"We have no good pictures of the other animals we saw on the hill. Our best picture is of Tess!"
said Peter.

51

"I know what to do now," said Mum. "Let's send this picture of Tess to the museum."

"Yes, we all really like the picture of Tess," said Peter.

"We looked for other animals, but Tess was the best!" said Jane.

New Key Words

Answer these questions about
the story.

1 What animal do Jane and Peter
   try to take a picture of first?

2 What animals do the children see
   as they walk up the hill?

3 What does Tess do when she sees
   the rabbits?

4 How do you think Peter and Jane
   feel on the train back to the city?

5 What is Jane and Peter's best
   picture at the end of the story?